CRUNCH and CRACK, OINK and WHACK!

ONOMATOPOEIA:
(AH-nuh-MAH-tuh-PEE-uh)
the naming of a thing or an action by
imitating or mimicking its sound, as in
BEEP, MOO, and **SPLASH**

CRUNCH and CRACK, OINK and WHACK!

AN ONOMATOPOEIA STORY

Brian P. Cleary   illustrated by **Pablo Pino**

Millbrook Press/Minneapolis

It's **ONOMATOPOEIA DAY** in Ms. Garcia's class
at Clip-Clop Country School for Girls and Boys.
The buses, cars, and kids arrive
in groups of three or four and five.

The hallways **HUM** and **BUZZ** with all their noise.

One day every year, the students go out on a hunt—
a favorite exercise of Ms. Garcia—
to search the grounds and school
for something interesting and cool:
it's what is known as onomatopoeia.

Onomatopoeia is a special kind of word
that imitates the sound of what is named.
BANG is one and so is **BUZZ**,
and **CLICK** and **SNAP** and **CLANG** because
the words and how they sound are much the same.

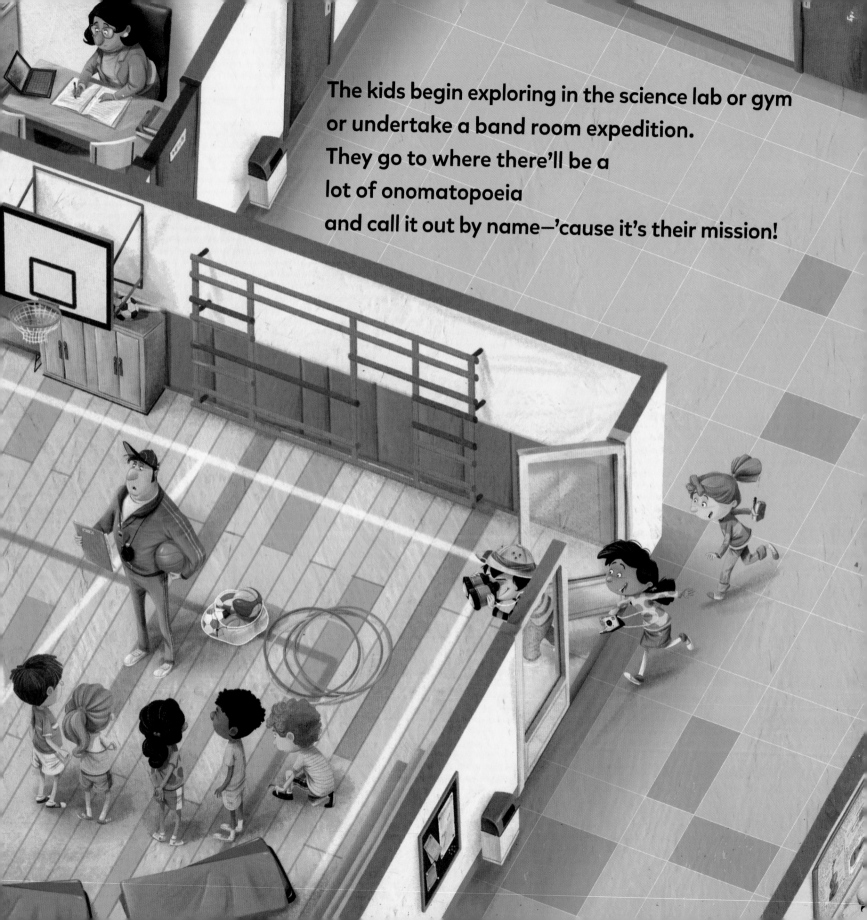

The kids begin exploring in the science lab or gym
or undertake a band room expedition.
They go to where there'll be a
lot of onomatopoeia
and call it out by name—'cause it's their mission!

The school is tucked among a brook,
a meadow, and a farm
that's home to chickens, goats,
and cows and sheep.

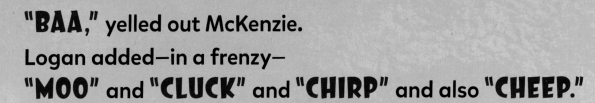

"**BAA,**" yelled out McKenzie.
Logan added—in a frenzy—
"**MOO**" and "**CLUCK**" and "**CHIRP**" and also "**CHEEP.**"

"**BABBLE,**" called out Alex as she peered into the brook,
then "**FLUTTER**" as she spied a butterfly.

"QUACK," said Isla, loudly,
as Dakota pointed proudly
and said "HONK" just as a goose was passing by.

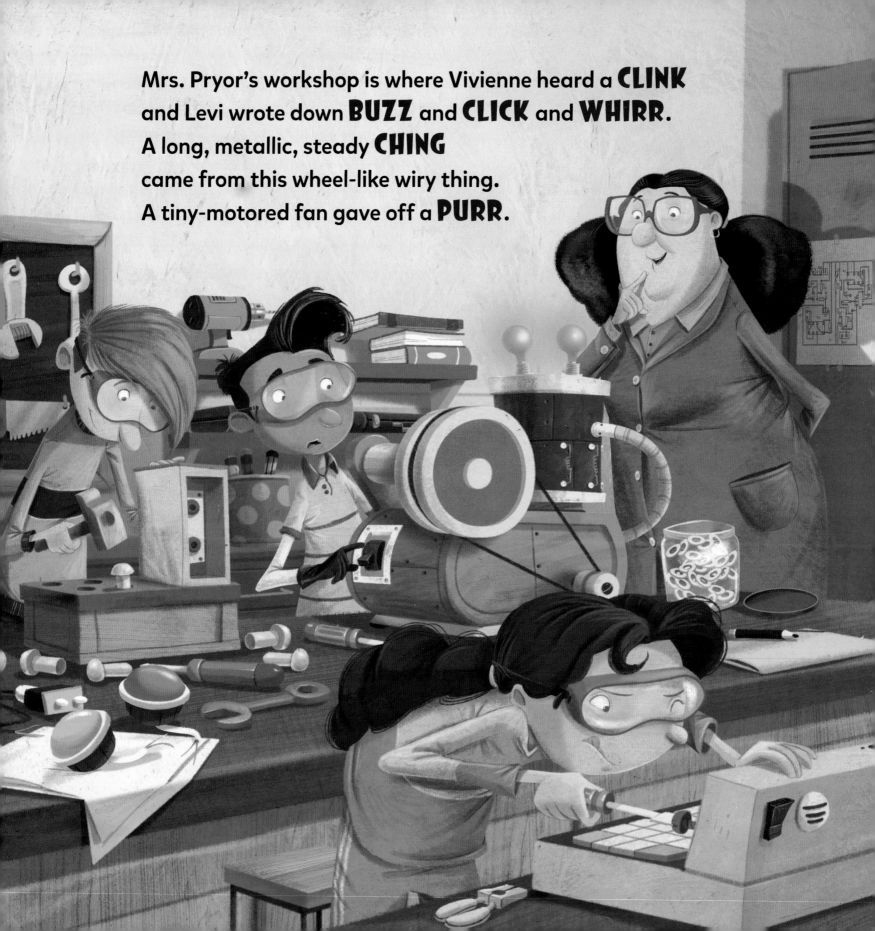

Mrs. Pryor's workshop is where Vivienne heard a **CLINK**
and Levi wrote down **BUZZ** and **CLICK** and **WHIRR**.
A long, metallic, steady **CHING**
came from this wheel-like wiry thing.
A tiny-motored fan gave off a **PURR**.

Outside Mr. Hernan's room, Fiona noted **TWANG**,
a **RAT-TAT-TAT**, a **BREET**, and **OOMPAH-PAH**,
a **JINGLE**, **JANGLE**, **TOOT**, and **TAP**,
a **BLARE**, a **RATTLE**, **TING**, and **CLAP**,
a **PLINK**, a **PLUNK**, a **BOOM**, and **WAH-WAH-WAH**.

Lily racked up several more inside the gym that day, like **DRIBBLE**, **BOUNCE**, and **SWISH** and **CRUNCH** and **CRACK**.

FWOOSH as tennis balls were hit.
THUD when baseballs reached a mitt.
Then later, **HUFF** and **PUFF** and
WHIFF and **WHACK**.

Just inside the restroom is where Brooke detected **DRIP** and **PING** and **SPUTTER**, also **SPLASH** and **SPRINKLE**.

Pam said softly, **"SPATTER."** Then Avery, **"PITTER-PATTER,"** along with **"WHISPER, FIZZ,** and **FLUSH** and **TINKLE."**

Mrs. Joyce's science lab's where Brice observed a **GURGLE**, and Ruby heard a **HISS** come from the beakers. Both heard **SPURTS** and **RINGING** and the sound of timers **DINGING** and a high-pitched **SQUEAK** from Mrs. Joyce's sneakers.

Late that afternoon, the classroom had a **BUZZ** about it
when everyone, including Ms. Garcia,
gathered, sharing what they'd found—
each **ZIP** and **PLOP** and **SCREECHING** sound—
each captured bit of onomatopoeia.

The principal walked by and heard a **BELCH**, a **BRAY**, a **BURP**, **MEOW**, a **SHRIEK** and **GRUNT**, a **WHOOP** and **WHOOSH**.

When she heard the loudest screecher,
she assumed they had no teacher,
and she opened up the door and shouted

SHOOSH!

Listen Up! More Examples of Onomatopoeia

Animal Noises

ARF
BAA
BARK
BRAY
BUZZ
CHEEP
CHIRP
CLIP-CLOP
CLUCK
COCK-A-DOODLE-DOO
CUCKOO
GROWL
HISS
MEOW
MOO
NEIGH
OINK
PANT
PURR
QUACK
RIBBIT
SNIFF
TWEET
WARBLE
WOOF

Mechanical Noises

BANG
CHA-CHING
CHING
CLANG
CLANK
CLICK
CLINK
CREAK
DING
DING-DONG
FLUSH
GONG
JINGLE
TICK-TOCK
TINKLE
TOOT
VROOM
WHIRR
WHIZZ
ZIP

Human Noises

AHEM
BAWL
BELCH
BLURT
BURP
CHATTER
CLAP
GARGLE
GASP
GIGGLE
GRUNT
GURGLE
HICCUP
HUM
MUMBLE
MURMUR
SCREECH
SHOOSH
SLAP
SLURP
SNAP
THUD
THUMP
WHIFF
WHISPER

Water Noises

DRIP
DRIZZLE
SPLASH
SPLISH-SPLASH
SPRINKLE

Miscellaneous Noises

BAM
CLATTER
CRACKLE
CRUNCH
FIZZ
FLUTTER
FWOOSH
KABOOM
PLOP
POP
PUFF
SPLAT
SWISH
SWOOSH
WHIP
WHOOSH

Further Reading

Blaisdell, Bette. *A Mouthful of Onomatopoeia*. North Mankato, MN: Capstone Press, 2014.
Discover many examples of onomatopoeia in this photo-filled book.

Bluemle, Elizabeth. *Tap Tap Boom Boom*. Somerville, MA: Candlewick, 2014.
Experience a New York City thunderstorm through onomatopoeia.

Gibson, Amy. *Split! Splat!* New York: Scholastic, 2012.
A girl and her dog explore all the drips, drops, and splats of rain.

McCanna, Tim. *Watersong*. New York: Simon & Schuster Books for Young Readers, 2017.
Join a fox as he seeks shelter from a noisy rainstorm.

Millbrook Press
A division of Lerner Publishing Group, Inc.
241 First Avenue North
Minneapolis, MN 55401 USA

For reading levels and more information, look up this title at www.lernerbooks.com.

Designed by Kimberly Morales.
Main body text set in Mikado medium 17/25.
Typeface provided by HVD Fonts.
The illustrations in this book were created with pencil and colored digitally
using Photoshop.

Library of Congress Cataloging-in-Publication Data

Names: Cleary, Brian P., 1959- author. | Pino, Pablo, 1981- illustrator.
Title: Crunch and crack, oink and whack! : an onomatopoeia story / text, Brian P.
    Cleary ; illustrations, Pablo Pino.
Description: Minneapolis, MN : Millbrook Press, a division of Lerner Publishing
    Group, Inc., [2019] | Summary: Illustrations and simple, rhyming text follow
    Ms. Garcia's class on a hunt in and around school for examples of onomatopoeia—
    words that imitate the sound of what they name. | Includes bibliographical
    references.
Identifiers: LCCN 2018008682 (print) | LCCN 2018016016 (ebook) |
    ISBN 9781541543775 (eb pdf) | ISBN 9781467787994 (lb : alk. paper)
Subjects: | CYAC: Stories in rhyme. | Sounds, Words for—Fiction. | Schools—Fiction.
Classification: LCC PZ8.3.C555 (ebook) | LCC PZ8.3.C555 Cru 2018 (print) |
    DDC [E]—dc23

LC record available at https://lccn.loc.gov/2018008682

Manufactured in the United States of America
1-38027-19817-8/22/2018